Books by Scott Corbett

The Trick Books

THE LEMONADE TRICK

THE MAILBOX TRICK

THE DISAPPEARING DOG TRICK

THE LIMERICK TRICK

THE BASEBALL TRICK

THE TURNABOUT TRICK

THE HAIRY HORROR TRICK

THE HATEFUL PLATEFUL
TRICK

THE HOME RUN TRICK

THE HOCKEY TRICK

THE BLACK MASK TRICK

THE HANGMAN'S GHOST
TRICK

Suspense Stories

COP'S KID

TREE HOUSE ISLAND

DEAD MAN'S LIGHT

CUTLASS ISLAND

ONE BY SEA

THE BASEBALL BARGAIN

THE MYSTERY MAN

DEAD BEFORE DOCKING

RUN FOR THE MONEY

THE CASE OF THE GONE
GOOSE

THE CASE OF THE FUGITIVE
FIREBUG

THE CASE OF THE TICKLISH
TOOTH

THE CASE OF THE SILVER
SKULL

THE CASE OF THE BURGLED
BLESSING BOX

Easy-to-Read Adventures

DR. MERLIN'S MAGIC SHOP

THE GREAT CUSTARD PIE
PANIC

THE BOY WHO WALKED
ON AIR

THE GREAT MCGONIGGLE'S
GRAY GHOST

THE GREAT MCGONIGGLE'S KEY
PLAY

THE GREAT MCGONIGGLE RIDES
SHOTGUN

What Makes It Work?

WHAT MAKES A CAR GO?

WHAT MAKES A TV WORK?

WHAT MAKES A LIGHT
GO ON?

WHAT MAKES A PLANE FLY?

WHAT MAKES A BOAT FLOAT?

Ghost Stories

THE RED ROOM RIDDLE

HERE LIES THE BODY

CAPTAIN BUTCHER'S BODY

THE HANGMAN'S GHOST TRICK

THE
HANGMAN'S GHOST
TRICK

by SCOTT CORBETT
Illustrated by Paul Galdone

An Atlantic Monthly Press Book

Little, Brown and Company   Boston · Toronto

FIRST EDITION

T10/77

Library of Congress Cataloging in Publication Data

Corbett, Scott.
  The hangman's ghost trick.

  "Atlantic-Monthly Press book."
  SUMMARY: Kevin and Kerby go to scary Bald Mountain at night to search for a rare mystery ingredient that would guarantee the prize in a cookie contest.
  [1. Humorous stories] I. Galdone, Paul. II. Title.
PZ7.C79938Han   [Fic]   77–23021
ISBN 0–316–15728–7

ATLANTIC–LITTLE, BROWN BOOKS
ARE PUBLISHED BY
LITTLE, BROWN AND COMPANY
IN ASSOCIATION WITH
THE ATLANTIC MONTHLY PRESS

Published simultaneously in Canada
by Little, Brown & Company (Canada) Limited

PRINTED IN THE UNITED STATES OF AMERICA

to Alyna Tung-mei Chien
with love from
your honorary grandfather

I

LATE ONE AFTERNOON on a warm summer day, Kerby
Maxwell and Fenton Claypool sat on the steps of Kerby's front
porch fiddling with an old anagrams game. On the grass at
the edge of the terrace sat Kerby's dog, Waldo.

All three wore preoccupied looks. Though none of them was
ready to admit it, they were worried, even depressed.

"Where could he go?" muttered Fenton, unable to keep his
mind on the game.

"I wonder if she'll ever find him?" muttered Kerby.

"I'll bet not. Either he'll come home on his own, or . . ."

Next door to Kerby lived a widow named Mrs. Pembroke
and — until recently — her big yellow cat, Xerxes. Every chance
he got, Xerxes sneaked over into Waldo's yard, just to devil
him. Every chance Waldo got, he chased Xerxes back into his
own yard and up a big tree. Mrs. Pembroke thought it was all
Waldo's fault. Kerby thought Mrs. Pembroke was a pain in
the neck.

"Well, at least we won't have to listen to her talk baby talk
to him anymore," Kerby pointed out.

"If you ask me, we ought to be cheering," said Fenton.

Three days ago Xerxes had started acting funny. He walked around looking half asleep. Mrs. Pembroke rushed him to a veterinarian, Dr. Schmilhaus, who was unable to find anything wrong. He prescribed rest and a light diet for a few days.

Unlike most cats, Xerxes did not mind riding in a car. He liked to lie on the shelf behind the backseat where he could glare through the rear window at cars that came too close.

On the way home from Dr. Schmilhaus's animal hospital, as they were driving through a hilly, wooded section on the outskirts of town, a black cat streaked across the road, causing Mrs. Pembroke to jam on the brakes and come to a stop. Upon reaching the side of the road the black cat turned and uttered a peculiar yowl.

At that moment Xerxes suddenly leaped out the window and raced away after the black cat, up the hillside and into the woods.

Not only had his frantic owner searched for him then and there, she had been back a couple of times each day to walk all over the hillside — and Mrs. Pembroke was a short, plump woman who hated walking. But it was all to no avail. Xerxes was gone.

"Well, it serves her right, she's such an old sourpuss," growled Kerby.

"That's right," agreed Fenton. "Why, if it was anybody but

her I'd probably offer to ride out there and help look for him, but —"

"Sure — but not for her, and who needs a stupid old cat like Xerxes around, anyway?"

Even as he was saying this Kerby was looking at Waldo and knowing darn well who needed Xerxes.

Dogs hate to have any changes made in their way of life. Xerxes was part of Waldo's daily routine. Checking constantly to make sure Xerxes had not sneaked through the hedge kept him on his toes and provided him with healthy exercise. There was nothing he enjoyed more than chasing Xerxes back into his own yard. There was nothing Xerxes enjoyed more than racing ahead of Waldo and clawing his way up the side of the big tree over there, because Xerxes was very vain about his tree-climbing abilities and liked to show them off.

Mrs. Pembroke never understood any of this.

Fenton was rearranging some of the anagram letters. He was very good at anagrams. The only trouble was that his set was old and battered and his sister had lost some of the letters. Still, there were enough left to fool around with when you had something on your mind and couldn't think of anything else to do.

"Look, I've got another word," he said, and laid out SERAPE.

"What's that, Fenton?"

"It's a kind of blanket Mexicans carry on one shoulder."

"You know more darn words!"

Kerby spoke enviously but not resentfully, because Fenton was never arrogant, never made you feel dumb because you didn't know as much as he did. Out of his letters — PESRTIACSEHT — Fenton had already made a lot of words, including SCRAP, PESTER, STEEP, SPIRE, STRETCH, RETCH, PRICE, CREST, and THREE, and might have made a lot more, except that Kerby was tired of anagrams, tired of thinking about a cat he didn't even like, and tired of watching Waldo sit around looking bored.

"Hey, let's do something else," he said, and jumped to his feet. "Come on, Waldo, let's have a wrestle."

Waldo stood up and made a feeble jump at him and they went to the ground together. Fenton, a tall, thin figure with very straight shoulders, came down from the porch and stood watching in his solemn way. But it was a halfhearted romp, and they gave it up as a car pulled to the curb next door. They watched Mrs. Pembroke get out.

Normally they would have disappeared, to avoid having to speak to her, but this time they just stood there, shocked by her appearance. Instead of her normal plump, bouncy, fussy self, she looked sad and older and sort of shrunken. Kerby watched her come around the car and start up her front steps, and confounded himself by suddenly blurting out a few words.

"I'm sorry about Xerxes, Mrs. Pembroke," he said.

"So am I, Mrs. Pembroke," said Fenton.

She looked up at them in utter astonishment, and then her eyes filled with tears.

"Thank you, boys," she said, and hurried on up the steps and into her house.

Kerby turned away, embarrassed to death by a lot of feelings he didn't want to feel and certainly didn't want to show.

"Darn it, this is getting on my nerves!" he complained, and he was really angry.

"Same here," said Fenton. "I'm sick of it. I wish there was something we could do. It's like a morgue around here!"

"What's a morgue?"

"It's a place full of dead bodies."

"A what? Listen, you don't think Xerxes is dead, do you?"

"Who knows? He might as well be, the way things are." Fenton sat down on the steps, glanced at them, muttered, *"Steps —* that's another word I could make," and then got a brooding look on his long, thin face. "Listen, I've been thinking about something . . ."

"What?"

"You know where Mrs. Pembroke told your mother Xerxes jumped out?"

"You mean out on Kotula Drive?"

"Yes — on Kotula between Carlsen Circle and Safford Street."

"Sure, I know. What about it?"

"Do you remember when we went with Mrs. Graymalkin out to Bald Mountain Road?"

"Sure!" Kerby shivered a little at the thought of it. They had traveled up that strange road with her before — once on a scary Halloween.

"Well, we got there from Kotula Drive. We passed Carlsen Circle, and I'm practically sure we turned off onto Bald Mountain Road before we came to Safford Street."

Kerby was suddenly excited. He sat down beside Fenton and stared at him.

"Are you sure?"

"Almost. But I'll tell you another funny thing."

"What?"

Fenton's voice dropped.

"I've been doing a little detective work. Yesterday at the library I happened to notice the city directory on one of the tables," he said, sounding as if he hadn't just *happened* to notice it at all. "So I looked to see if Bald Mountain Road was listed in the street guide."

He shook his head.

"It wasn't."

They exchanged a long, thoughtful look. Then Fenton continued.

"So next I looked at the official street map. I looked everywhere up and down Kotula Drive, especially between Carlsen Circle and Safford Street."

Again he shook his head.

8

"No Bald Mountain Road. No Bald Mountain Road anywhere. It's mighty funny."

"It sure is!"

"But I don't care what the map says, it's got to be along there somewhere. Near where Xerxes jumped out."

They exchanged another long look. Then they took a look around them. The sun had set, the first hint of dusk was in the air.

"So I was thinking . . ."

"You're right," said Kerby. "Come on, Waldo!"

And without another word they headed down the street for Peterson Park.

2

PETERSON PARK was a small public park not far away. It was full of trees and bushes, which were full of squirrels and birds, and in some parts rugged stone outcroppings hung over the pleasant paths rambling through the park.

It was here, one memorable afternoon when the shadows were growing long and dark under the trees, that Kerby had met Mrs. Graymalkin.

He had been hurrying along a path, late for supper, when ahead of him at the drinking fountain a strange sight greeted his eyes.

An old lady wearing a black hat with an enormous black feather drooping from it, a straggly black cape over a straggly black dress, and shoes with ridiculously high heels, was standing there with one heel caught in the drain beside the drinking fountain.

She asked Kerby for help. He worked the shoe loose for her. Out of gratitude she brought him, the next afternoon, a Feats O' Magic chemistry set that had once belonged to her own son Felix.

Since then, thanks to Mrs. Graymalkin and the chemistry set, the boys and Waldo had lived through many astonishing experiences, some of them hair-raising. But if anyone was likely to be able to help out in the present situation, they felt it would be Mrs. Graymalkin.

When daylight was growing dim under the trees was just the time they could expect to find her. Sure enough, alongside the park a tall, gaunt antique sedan stood at the curb.

"There's Nostradamus!" cried Kerby. "We're in luck!"

Nostradamus was the name Mrs. Graymalkin had given to her ancient automobile. Many a wild ride they had had in the old relic! Seeing it there, they knew she was taking her constitutional, as she called her walk through the park. Kerby stopped to admire the car and pat one of its floppy fenders.

"It's darn funny to me that Bald Mountain Road isn't even on the map," he said, preparing to enjoy himself at Fenton's expense. "Nostradamus certainly never had any trouble getting us there. And when I think of that crazy old cottage her friend Dame Whirley lives in, with that spooky black cat of hers — Say! Speaking of black cats, you don't suppose . . ."

"Now don't start making things up," snapped Fenton. "Just because a black cat ran across the road! . . ."

Kerby knew he had touched a sore spot with Fenton, whose firm belief in science left no room for doings of an occult or supernatural nature. Kerby knew, and as usual made the most of it.

"Well, if you want to believe science can explain everything Mrs. Graymalkin and Dame Whirley do, go right ahead, but *I* still think they're a couple of —"

"Witches don't exist, I tell you! I'll admit Mrs. Graymalkin knows more science than the scientists do, but that's all! Now, come on, we're wasting time!"

Grinning wickedly, Kerby followed his indignant friend down the slope into the park. Waldo had already romped on ahead, accepting the challenge of a resident squirrel to a footrace. He had disappeared from sight. The boys headed for the path at the bottom of the slope, but they had not yet reached it when a raspy croak startled them.

"Lackaday!"

They skidded to a halt.

"Dear little Waldo! Oh, lackaday!"

Seated off to one side on a large rock in a small grove of trees was Mrs. Graymalkin, and she was patting Waldo on the head. The sight of her would have sent the average dog racing away with his tail between his legs, but she and Waldo were old friends. He was looking up at her with concern, since it was obvious she was not happy with life.

"Hi, Mrs. Graymalkin!"

"Why, Kerby! And Fenton!" She gave them a snaggle-toothed smile, but its normal gaiety was missing. "It's a comfort to see you in my hour of woe!"

The boys' spirits plummeted. Instead of doing something to

relieve their depression, Mrs. Graymalkin looked ready to add to it.

"Gee, Mrs. Graymalkin, what's the matter?"

"Matter enough, Kerby, matter enough indeed!" she keened, and heaved a sigh that made the long black ornament on her hat droop like the tail feathers of a dying swan. "Dear boys, I have been tricked and trapped!"

"Trapped?"

"Aye, trapped! Trapped in an intolerable situation, for which I shall pay dearly!"

The boys exchanged a startled glance. This sounded serious, much more serious than their own problem.

"Gosh, Mrs. Graymalkin, what did you do?"

Another sigh agitated the feather and ruffled the shimmery surface of the black cape — which, in deference to summer temperatures, seemed to be made of some lightweight material.

"Well, to begin with, let me explain that I have a small circle of friends — Dame Whirley is one of them — with whom I often spend a social evening. You might call it a — well, a club, since we have a great many common interests."

Kerby darted a glance at Fenton which was coldly received. Fenton knew well enough what kind of circle Kerby had in mind, a circle his own scientific mind was not prepared to accept.

"Now, among our circle is a person who has been a rival of mine for ages and ages, ever since the days of — But never

15

mind that, the point is that we are forever trying to get the better of one another, I and Dame — But the name does not matter, either . . ."

"Not Dame Whirley?"

"Mercy, no! She is my dearest friend. No, this is another Dame — she claims the title, though I might add I have never been convinced she came by her dameship honestly. However, let us hasten on to the tragedy. Now, one of the areas in which we have always been keen rivals is that of the culinary arts."

"The what?"

"The culinary arts. Cooking!"

At once a strange picture sprang up in Kerby's mind, a picture of Mrs. Graymalkin and her rival each bending over a steaming pot, stirring mysterious ingredients round and round while muttering weird incantations. Was that the kind of cooking she meant?

"She was constantly puffing herself up about her superb secret recipes, and claiming supremacy in the field, until finally I could stand it no longer and decided to put her in her place."

"How?"

"In one of our meetings I challenged her openly to a test of skills, and offered to make any wager she cared to suggest on the outcome."

"What did she say to that?"

"Well, she wiggled out of it. She said she would be glad to give me a much-needed lesson, except that such a contest would be impossible because none of the members of our circle would be acceptable as impartial judges. For this she was laughed to scorn, but she obstinately maintained her opinion, and there the matter stood. I had gained an easy victory — or so I thought.

"For a long time nothing more was said about cooking, but then a week ago, she suddenly swooped into one of our meetings with a wild expression of sly triumph on her face. 'Now we shall see who laughs last!' she shrieked. 'Now it's I who challenge *you*, Goodwife Graymalkin! At last I have found some absolutely impartial judges for our battle of the pots and pans!' And with that she produced a copy of the evening newspaper and waggled it offensively under my nose. 'The Curious Cookie Contest!' she cried."

Cookies! Kerby almost laughed out loud. After the kind of steaming concoctions *he* had been thinking of, cookies sounded silly.

"Are you boys aware of the contest currently being conducted by our local newspaper? The Curious Cookie Contest?"

"Sure," said Kerby. "Mom was talking about it the other night. Dad told her she ought to enter her fudge brownies, but she said there's nothing curious about them."

"My mother was talking about it, too," said Fenton. "Isn't the idea that the cookie recipe anyone sends in is supposed to have one nutty thing in it?"

Mrs. Graymalkin winced at his choice of words.

" 'Nutty'? What sort of language is that, Fenton? One 'mystery ingredient' is how the newspaper put it," she reminded them with a touch of asperity in her manner. "I must admit I find your choice of terms doubly painful — yes, doubly so — because it was a nut that caused my downfall."

"Anyone we know?" asked Kerby.

She gave him a sharply reproving glance.

"I am not referring to a person, Kerby, I am referring to an actual nut, from a tree. But more of that later. My immediate reaction was one of disdain.

" 'What? Enter a public contest? Allow my name to appear in the newspapers? Don't be vulgar,' I retorted, but she only tossed her head in a particularly obnoxious manner.

" 'Never fear, your name won't appear, because you shan't win! *I* shall!' she cried with ridiculous assurance.

"Then it occurred to me that the foolish woman had played straight into my hands — because when it came to cookies I was invincible. It so happened I possessed a secret cookie recipe so superior to anything she might produce that it would provide a way out of my difficulties, a way to avoid any public display."

"Great!" said Kerby. "How —"

"In a moment, in a moment," said Mrs. Graymalkin, holding up her hand. "While I was turning all this over in my mind, she continued to press what she thought to be her advantage.

" 'You once claimed you were ready to wager anything on the outcome of a contest between us,' she sneered. 'Well, if

18

you meant it, then I am ready to wager my incomparable cat Cagliostro against that old broken-down sedan of yours — Nostradamus!' "

"N-Nostradamus?"

Kerby began to have an uneasy feeling in the pit of his stomach. Could it be that . . . ?

"My plan was simple," said Mrs. Graymalkin. "Once I had tested my recipe and made certain all was in order, I would suggest a preview of our entries amongst our own circle. The matchless quality of my cookies would be so unmistakable that even her supporters within our group would be forced to admit their superiority. Magnanimous in victory, I would release her from her wager — I don't like that old cat of hers and wouldn't even take him as a *gift,* to tell the truth — and I would thus heap coals of fire on her head. My triumph would be complete.

"And with this glowing vision in mind, I accepted her challenge. My dinglenuts would make me invincible!"

"Your *what?*"

"Dinglenuts."

The boys gaped at each other.

"I've never heard of dinglenuts," said Fenton.

"I can well believe that," said Mrs. Graymalkin, her eyelids drooping slyly. "Few have. They have been a well-guarded secret for centuries. It takes them years and years to grow, and when they are finally mature and ready for use each little dinglenut is no larger than the head of a wooden match. Naturally this means that a dinglenut harvest is a great deal of work — and shelling them is no simple task, either."

"I'll bet not!" said Fenton. "They don't sound as if they'd be worth the trouble."

"So it would seem, so it would seem," said Mrs. Graymalkin, nodding. "When eaten as nuts, even when salted, they are totally uninteresting, and tend to get between the teeth in a most uncomfortable manner," she said, causing Kerby to suppress a grin, because even a Brazil nut would have had trouble getting caught in the gaps between Mrs. Graymalkin's few remaining teeth.

One bony finger shot into the air, indicating that the point of her story had been reached.

"However!" she croaked. "However, when they are added to a certain cookie recipe I happen to know — a recipe which is perfectly standard in every other way — something happens to them. All I can tell you is, they make the most delicious cookies you or anybody else ever tasted! I call them Dinglenut Puffs."

Again the finger stabbed the air.

"And!" she cried. "And — I happened to have the only remaining supply of dinglenuts from the last harvest!"

"Wow!"

"So home I went, sifted flour, measured sugar, sliced butter, and then took out my precious little bag of dinglenuts."

20

She paused, almost unable to continue, but then got hold of herself and went on.

"Oh, that wicked woman! I am undone! My dinglenuts were shriveled and dry beyond redemption!"

"You mean, no good?"

"Hopeless!"

"But, gee, can't you get some more?"

Mrs. Graymalkin shook her head impatiently at such ignorance.

"In the first place, they grow only in one spot on a single mountaintop in a remote corner of Transylvania, far across the sea. In the second place, there is only one harvest every seventy years, and the next one is not due for another three years."

"What?" Fenton was so astonished that his large cup-handle ears seemed to waggle. "You mean to say those nuts you have are sixty-seven years old? I'd think they *would* dry up in that time!"

"You might think so, but they wouldn't," replied Mrs. Graymalkin tartly, "not unless they were made to dry up!"

"*Made* to?"

"Aye, made to! Oh, how did that woman ever learn my secret, and how did she cause my dinglenuts to dwindle, peak, and pine? Of course, I shouldn't be surprised, knowing her as I do to be a consummate mistress of the black arts — speaking figuratively, of course, a mere figure of speech," she added hastily, though not before a startled glance had passed between the boys. "So that is the sad, sad story, and that is why you find me so lone and lorn, so worn and wan. If I lose Nostradamus — and *she* will never return *him,* of that you may be sure! — I shan't be able to come here anymore for my beloved constitutionals!"

By now Kerby and Fenton were looking worn and wan themselves, not to say pale and trembling. If she were no longer able to take her constitutionals, they might never meet her again! Their threatened losses were mounting unbearably. First Xerxes, next Nostradamus, and now — maybe even Mrs. Graymalkin herself!

3

KERBY WAS PLUNGED into despair. Fenton's naturally long face extended itself to new limits. Waldo lay down and looked like a small, shaggy sheep dog mourning beside his master's grave. Life seemed to be coming apart at the seams.

Many a time had Mrs. Graymalkin helped them. More than once had they helped her. They were quick to offer their services now.

"Is there anything we can do?" asked Fenton.

"Just name it," said Kerby stoutly.

"Thank you, boys, thank you," said Mrs. Graymalkin, obviously touched. "I only wish there were, because I know how well I can depend on you. As for dear little Waldo, he has certainly proved on many occasions that his loyalty is beyond question," she added, causing Waldo to sit up in order to throw out his chest.

"Are you *sure* there is nothing you can do to make the dingle-nuts okay again?" asked Kerby. "Gee, my mother soaks dried navy beans overnight and the next day they're as good as new and ready to bake!"

But their friend shook her head sadly.

"Kerby, I have searched through every ancient cookbook in my collection — and it is an impressive one if I do say so myself — I have tried every broth, brew, and bromide I could think of, but it is hopeless. I am afraid I am beaten."

"Well, I think it was rotten of that old rival of yours to cast a spell over your dinglenuts!"

"Cast a spell? What a funny, old-fashioned way of putting it, Kerby! To say that she 'gave them the business' would be more in keeping with modern parlance," said Mrs. Graymalkin, and changed the subject. "But enough of my troubles. Now tell me what brought you here," she said, making an admirable effort to shift her attention. "I could tell at once that you, too, are carrying some heavy burden. What is it?"

"Well . . ." Compared to hers, their problem seemed small. Still, she had asked . . .

"It's Xerxes," said Fenton.

"Xerxes? That interesting cat who lives with Kerby's troublesome neighbor?"

"Yes, ma'am."

"Well, well, well! And what has Xerxes been up to now?"

"He's disappeared."

"Vanished?"

"Yes, ma'am."

"When? Tell me all about it."

Quickly Fenton explained.

"And the reason we came over to look for you," he concluded, "is that as near as we can figure, Xerxes jumped out of the car somewhere very close to —"

"Bald Mountain Road!" said Mrs. Graymalkin, never slow on the uptake. "Mercy me, it does sound quite possible, does it not? Yes, indeed, indeed, indeed!"

Fenton gave her a guarded glance.

"It's funny, though," he said. "I went to the library and looked in the city directory and couldn't find Bald Mountain Road anywhere. I couldn't find it on the city maps, either."

"Ah, yes — well, those maps are so haphazard, so poorly done, to be sure," said Mrs. Graymalkin airily. "They leave out a great deal. Actually, Dame Whirley is the only person who lives along that road, and she does value her privacy. She goes to considerable lengths to protect it. Nevertheless, *we* know where the road is, don't we, Fenton, dear?" she asked, and her old blue eyes twinkled at him from their cobweb nests of wrinkles and crow's-feet.

"Well, yes, we do," admitted Fenton, looking away with a flustered expression that amused Kerby greatly.

"Well, now, let us see, let us see," said Mrs. Graymalkin, bending her mind to the problem. "Xerxes had been acting strangely, you say . . ."

"Yes. He looked half asleep all the time."

"So your neighbor took him to Dr. Schmilhaus for a checkup. Yes, yes, yes — well, Schmilhaus is a good man, within veterinary limits, but of course he knows nothing of the more subtle workings of the feline physiology and psychology, nothing at all. Naturally *he* could find nothing wrong. But then, on the way home, Xerxes suddenly leapt from the car window and raced away up the hill and into the woods, did he? Near Bald Mountain Road. Hmm! A big yellow cat . . . yellow, yellow, yellow —"

All at once a strange light flashed in the bright old eyes, and once again a bony finger stabbed the air.

"Siena seed!" cried Mrs. Graymalkin.

"What seed?"

"Siena seed! Of course! Cats know what they need, cats are their own best physicians. Xerxes' keen nostrils may have caught a whiff of the plant medicine he craved, or the black cat, sensing his condition — cats are *very* mysterious — may have informed him —"

Again she stopped in mid-sentence. This time she was so surprised and excited she popped her hand over her mouth. When she took it away it was plain that some new hope was flickering, however feebly.

"My Aunt Edith's siena seed cookies! Not in a class with my dinglenut puffs, to be sure, but then beggars cannot be choosers . . ."

The boys were bewildered.

"What are you talking about, Mrs. Graymalkin?"

26

"My Aunt Edith! She was a great favorite of mine, and a superb cook. I was even named after her."

The news was astounding. Somehow they had never thought of the fact that Mrs. Graymalkin might have a first name like everybody else.

"You mean, your name is —?"

"Yes, indeed. Thanks to her, I am Edith T. Graymalkin."

Wonder upon wonder! Not only a first name, but a middle initial as well!

"Hoity-toity! I had quite forgotten that recipe she was good enough to give me so long, long ago! Yes, yes, and the key is Xerxes. Find Xerxes and we may well find some of the precious siena seed — because I feel almost certain that was what lured him out of the car."

"Gee! How do you know that?"

Mrs. Graymalkin's eyelids went again into one of their sly droops.

"It so happens I have some little knowledge of the cat world, and I know that cats employ an astonishing number of rare herbs, seeds, and grasses as cures for certain feline ailments — ailments that poor workaday practitioners such as Schmilhaus never heard of. Now, from the sound of it — his being a *yellow* cat, that is; that's a significant point — poor Xerxes may well be suffering from a catatonic condition, and the cat tonic for *that* is — siena seed!"

"Wow! You mean, the same stuff you need for your Aunt Edith's cookies?"

"The very same. Yes, yes, yes, we may be on the track of something crucial here! I must go home at once, because there is work to do, work to do!" cried Mrs. Graymalkin, and now the long black feather on her hat was dancing a tentative jig of hope. "I must get out Aunt Edith's recipe and look it over carefully. Then I must delve into my books and refresh my memory as to the exact growing conditions required for the shy little plant, unknown to conventional botanists — *Pimpinella troglodytes,* more commonly known as frightweed, from which siena seed may be collected."

Mrs. Graymalkin looked down at the boys eagerly.

"Are you free tomorrow evening?"

"Well," said Fenton, "tomorrow is Friday —"

"And," said Kerby, "they let us go to the movies Friday night —"

"So," said Fenton, "we could skip the movie —"

"Splendid, splendid, splendid! Then a-hunting we will go, and if we can find Xerxes we may be able to solve all our problems in one grand sweep!"

"But are you sure your aunt's cookies can win the contest, Mrs. Graymalkin?" Fenton asked anxiously.

His anxiety proved well founded.

"No," she admitted. "Not as certain as I would have been with my dinglenut puffs — but at least I'll have a chance, which

28

is more than I had before your fortunate arrival! Oh, and by the way, will dear little Waldo be able to come, too?"

Waldo danced up on his hind legs, all eagerness. He certainly didn't have anything on for Friday night, not being a moviegoer. His calendar was clear.

"Sure, I don't see why not," said Kerby.

"Then do bring him along. Who knows — he may be of help in tracking down poor Xerxes! Meet me here as soon as you have finished supper and we shall see what we shall see. Now off we go, each his own way — tomorrow is another day!"

4

WHEN THEY REACHED the park Friday evening Nostradamus was standing in his customary place at the curb and Mrs. Graymalkin was sitting at the wheel. She gave them a wave and a gap-toothed smile.

"Well, well, well, good evening, boys, and dear little Waldo!" she cried. "I'm glad to see you were able to come. Jump in, jump in, there's much to do!"

Fenton opened a rear door of the antique sedan. Waldo scrambled in and took his usual seat by a window. As soon as the boys had settled themselves beside Waldo, Nostradamus began to heave and cough as though he were in the last stages of asthma. The passengers were not alarmed. The old car always started up in that fashion. With a jerk and a jounce they were on their way.

Even though they were not alarmed by the rattles and bangs of the venerable vehicle, they were excited and just a touch nervous at finding themselves once again on their way to Bald Mountain Road in Nostradamus.

30

"Did you find your aunt's recipe, Mr. Graymalkin?"

"Yes, indeed, thank you, Fenton. Whether it will be good enough to save Nosy remains to be seen," she said, and the old car seemed to give an extra shudder as she spoke, "but certainly — if only we can find a few pinches of siena seed — it seems our best hope."

"And did you find out anything about —"

"Yes, yes, indeed I did. Diligent research in several ancient botanical manuals convinced me that *Pimpinella troglodytes,* which grows only in certain small caves in certain restricted areas, is the plant a yellow cat suffering from a catatonic condition would seek out."

"But, gee, how can we find Xerxes? There's an awful lot of space up there on Bald Mountain!"

"Don't forget, Kerby, dear, we have an important clue to work with . . ."

Fenton caught on.

"Certain small caves in certain restricted areas!"

"Precisely, Fenton. Furthermore, we are fortunate in having a friend who lives on that very road, one who knows the area well. We shall stop at Dame Whirley's cottage and I shall consult with her for a few moments."

As she talked, Nostradamus was rattling along at a great rate. Fenton nudged Kerby and jerked his head toward the window. They were approaching Carlsen Circle on Kotula

Drive. They peered ahead through the fading light of the summer dusk. According to the city map the next street after Carlsen Circle, a good quarter of a mile beyond it, was Safford Street. There were no streets, roads, or lanes shown between them.

Nostradamus rattled on, and so did Mrs. Graymalkin.

"Dear Dame Whirley is a good friend, indeed. I am sure she will be most helpful to us in narrowing down our search. Ah, and here we are!"

She sent Nostradamus swooping in a wild curve onto a side road which had suddenly appeared with a signpost beside it that said —

"Bald Mountain Road!"

With a sort of strangled gulp Fenton blurted out the words. Mrs. Graymalkin cackled dryly.

"Fenton, Fenton, you must learn not to put too much trust in those inaccurate city maps. The persons who prepare them are often underpaid and poorly trained in their craft," she declared. "Let us simply be thankful we do not have to depend on them for our directions."

"Yes, ma'am!"

Subdued and thoughtful, the boys stared ahead up the winding road on which, almost at once, darkness seemed to rush down to meet them. Soon they rounded a bend and there sat a thatch-roofed cottage they had seen before, a crazily crooked cottage with a crazily crooked chimney.

"And here we are! Wait here, all of you — I'll be back in a trice!"

Mrs. Graymalkin stepped out of the car, teetered over to the cottage door, and knocked. It opened. She slipped inside. The door shut again with a bang.

Kerby and Fenton were alone in the night, with only Waldo and their goose pimples to keep them company.

For a while all was quiet except for the furtive rustle of the wind in the trees. The leaves seemed to be whispering dreadful secrets to one another. Kerby ran his tongue over dry lips.

"It sure did get dark in a hurry," he said.

"It always seems awful dark up here," said Fenton.

Then things livened up. From the cottage came sounds that were somewhere between chanting, caterwauling, and screeching. A huge white smoke ring puffed up from the chimney and was snatched away by the wind. The door opened a crack and a black cat shot out to race yowling around the house, three wild trips around it and then a dive inside, with the door slammed shut again.

"There's that black cat of Dame Whirley's," said Fenton.

"I'll bet that's the one Xerxes ran after," said Kerby.

Fenton did not reply. It was no easy struggle to cling to his customary scientific frame of mind on Bald Mountain Road. As for Waldo, he was looking out the window and shaking his head in a superior canine way. How any animal could do any-

thing so silly as to go yowling around a house three times lickety-split was beyond him. But then, what could anyone expect of a cat?

The cottage door opened again and out came Mrs. Graymalkin. She teetered back to the car in as matter-of-fact a manner as though she had merely been visiting some tourist information center.

"Well! I bring good news," she said, while the boys wondered how any good news could have been mixed in among all that chanting and caterwauling and screeching. But Fenton said politely, "I'm glad to hear it, Mrs. Graymalkin. What's the good news?"

"It is just as I had hoped. My dear friend definitely verifies the existence of small caves farther up the mountain. So on we go, on we go!"

5

NOSTRADAMUS COUGHED and sputtered into action and fender-flapped on up the rough road. Soon they were passing a cemetery, a place Kerby and Fenton had found it necessary to visit one memorable Halloween.

"H-how much farther, Mr. Graymalkin?" Kerby asked in a small voice.

"Oh, up around the base of Hangman's Knob," she replied in the cheery tones of someone mentioning Laguna Beach or Disneyland.

"Hangman's Kn-n-n-n-nob?"

"Oh, now, we mustn't let romantic old place-names bother us — must we, Fenton?" she trilled, casting a sly glance at them over her shoulder. "Goodness me, nobody's been hanged up there for ever so long! And certainly we don't intend to worry about trifles if we are going to locate poor Xerxes and let him lead us to our precious frightweed with its invaluable cargo of siena seed!"

Both boys scrunched down in their seats, and the faces they turned toward the windows were pale. Up and up they went,

farther than they had ever gone before. The rutted winding
lane was guarded by huge twisted trees whose gnarled limbs
were like bony-handed arms ready to snatch at them. This was
new territory, unknown to them. They would have preferred to
leave it that way.

Meanwhile Mrs. Graymalkin was peering out the window
and muttering to herself.

> *Skulls of scapegoats,*
> *One on three,*
> *At side of road*
> *The pile will be —*

"Ah, yes, there they are! Hard to pick out, I must say," she
declared as a small pile of ghoulish roundish objects shone dully
for an instant in the headlights.

> *Double beat*
> *Of pounding heart,*
> *Then 'tis time*
> *To stop and start!*

Kerby and Fenton furnished the double beat of pounding
heart without half trying. Mrs. Graymalkin seemed to know it,
too, because as she brought Nostradamus to a squealing stop she
whirled her head around to treat them to one of her gap-toothed
smiles.

"About here, wouldn't you say, boys? If my old ears didn't
deceive me, I believe I timed it about right. Now then, every-

body out! Everybody out and we will form our groups," she said, bustling out of the car like a camp director.

"Our g-groups?"

Fenton stepped gingerly into the darkness with Kerby close behind him and staying close. With Nostradamus's headlights turned off, the night seemed black as the inside of a tomb.

"Yes, yes, yes, we must divide our forces if we are to conquer. Divided we stand, united we fall," she said, making a little joke of it that did not get any laughs from her audience. "We are now at the base of Hangman's Knob and may begin our search. According to my information, if we circle the base we are almost certain to find a small cave somewhere along the way.

"Fenton and Kerby, you may strike out to the left, moving around the summit in a clockwise direction, whilst Waldo and I try our skills to the right, traveling in .a counterclockwise direction. With luck we should meet on the far side, having covered the entire circuit."

Kerby gulped.

"What if we aren't lucky?"

"Oh, goodness gracious, Kerby, dear, let us have no faint hearts here!" chirped Mrs. Graymalkin. "Instead, let us spring into action with our customary confidence. Come, Waldo — this way!"

And with that she teetered off down a narrow path with Waldo tail-wagging along behind her. They seemed gone in an instant. Kerby and Fenton were alone. Above them they could feel, more than see, the towering mass of the top, that sinister summit with the grisly name of Hangman's Knob. Kerby clung to one of the car door handles for reassurance. Even Nostradamus was company.

"I hope Nosy appreciates all we're going through for him!"

Fenton squared his already straight shoulders and took a deep breath.

"Let's go. Here's the path."

Taking one numb-footed step at a time they started along the path through the woods. Their eyes had adjusted to the dark now. They were able to see things, which almost made their ordeal worse, because now they could see little glimmers and gleams in the underbrush around them. Something squeaked and fluttered past their heads with the speed of black lightning.

"A bat!"

"Y-yes," said Fenton, and made a brave attempt to regain something of his scientific attitude. "Don't worry, we don't have vampire bats in this part of the world."

"What do you know about *this* part of the world?" retorted Kerby. "Yi!"

From somewhere behind them had come a shriek. It could have been the wail of a soul in torment or merely the complaint of some small animal being torn to pieces, it was hard to say which. Fenton favored the latter theory.

"That was p-probably an owl catching a mouse," he declared in the tones of a junior scientist wanting above all to convince himself. "Owls do much good work in keeping down the mouse population."

"Well, I wish they'd do it when I'm not here," said Kerby crossly, "and I hope Mrs. Graymalkin and Waldo are getting a move on. The sooner we meet the better!"

Fenton grabbed Kerby's arm and pointed ahead.

"Look, there are some rocky ledges! That's just the kind of place you might find a small cave."

The sudden prospect of success gave them courage to creep forward. The ledges were sufficiently in the open so that feeble hints of cloud-obscured moonlight made the limestone shimmer dull gray in the darkness. In a moment they could see a jagged black opening in the gray surface. A cave! Unquestionably a small cave. They stopped to nudge each other and point, then crept forward to the mouth of the cave.

In the blackness within, something glowed, something small, round, and red, and a dry hissing sound made them jump back.

"A snake!" gasped Kerby.

Fenton, trying to keep his head, quavered, "With one eye?"

"He's looking at us from one side!" was Kerby's opinion, and for him one eye was enough. He couldn't have stood two!

"Take it easy!" said Fenton. "Snakes don't attack if you don't force them to. Now, just back away slowly, one step at a time . . ."

They were backing away slowly like two half-paralyzed creatures, and hoping they would not see any red glow come out of the cave toward them, when a sudden rustle behind them made them leap like two jumping jacks.

"Mercy me, it's Kerby and Fenton!" cried a scratchy voice, snatching them back at the last instant from the brink of hysteria. "Oh, drat! Have we failed to find our cave?"

"Mrs. Graymalkin!"

"There's a cave right back there," reported Fenton.

"With a snake in it!" reported Kerby.

"Or something," said Fenton, not wishing to make an unscientific assumption.

"Well, well, well! Let me see!"

Mrs. Graymalkin hurried forward to the cave, accompanied by the rest of her group — and it was Waldo who, with his keener nostrils, caught a familiar scent. Peering into the cave he uttered an inquiring bark.

"R-r-r-uff?"

From within the cave came a plaintive sound.

"M-r-r-r-ow?"

"R-r-ruff!"

"M-r-r-r-ow!"

With that there was a slow scrabble of paws on pebbles, and a large, scrawny yellow cat walked stiffly out of the cave.

"It's Xerxes!" cried Kerby.

It was Xerxes, to be sure, and the small, round, red glowing object was Xerxes' nose.

6

FOR A MOMENT they all simply stared at the big cat. Then Waldo sat down abruptly and began making strange noises.

Mrs. Graymalkin reproved him sharply.

"Really, Waldo, it is not very nice of you to laugh at poor Xerxes when he's in such a predicament —"

"*Fssssst!*" agreed Xerxes, spitting at Waldo. He liked a joke as much as the next cat, but at the present time he was definitely not in the mood for one.

"Lackaday, I don't like this, I don't like this at all," said Mrs. Graymalkin. "I had no idea frightweed was able to produce any such side effects. . . . Poor Xerxes, I'll wager you're half starved," she added, and then revealed her usual forethought. From beneath her black cape she produced a small bowl and a carton of milk. Xerxes all but dived into the portion she poured out for him. The lapping of his tongue sounded like a small outboard motor. The glow from his nose made the milk look pink, but he was too hungry to care.

"What a beezer!" said Kerby. "Can you do something for it, Mrs. Graymalkin?"

She shook her head worriedly.

"At the moment I haven't the faintest idea whether *anything* can be done. This will mean long hours in my library. But in the meantime, now that we're here, we must search this cave and find the frightweed Xerxes has partaken of."

Again she had recourse to that amazing supply house she carried beneath her cape. This time she brought out a candle. She seemed to be a sleight-of-hand expert, too, because instantly the candle was lighted, and neither Kerby nor Fenton saw quite how she managed it.

"Now let's have a look."

She stooped and thrust the candle inside the low, narrow opening. The cave was indeed small.

"I'll crawl in and really look around," offered Fenton.

"No, I will, I'm smaller," said Kerby, feeling braver now. It seemed unlikely that Xerxes, not one to be sociable in the best of circumstances, would have been sharing his quarters with a snake. Holding the candle, Kerby crawled inside and inspected every inch of the cramped space.

"I can't see any weeds," he reported.

"What?" A heightened tone of alarm crackled in Mrs. Graymalkin's voice. "But it *must* be there! Surely he couldn't have eaten every scrap of it! Look, Kerby, look — we *must* find some! It will be a small, pale, colorless weed . . ."

Kerby literally put his nose into every corner, then came out and said, "Fenton, you try."

Fenton subjected the cave to a scientifically thorough search, but made the same report.

"There just aren't any weeds in there at all," he said, and glared at Xerxes. *"He* pigged down every bit of them!"

"Perhaps so, but we must not blame him. He was merely following the dictates of nature — and look at the price he has paid! And besides, perhaps all is not lost even now!"

"What do you mean?"

"Are we forgetting our special clue? Certain small caves in certain restricted areas? There may have been other small caves along our path which we overlooked — and we must search for them now as we have never searched before!"

For what seemed like hours they circled the base of Hangman's Knob, prying and poking into every inch of it. Even Xerxes came along. Obviously he felt that if there was any hope of curing his inflammation, that hope lay with his new friend.

They suffered from brambles and briars, nettles and nerves, but not another cave could they find that even a mouse could have crept into. When they had come full circle back to Xerxes' cave, there was nothing to do but admit defeat. Kerby and Fenton had never seen Mrs. Graymalkin more dejected.

"Mine enemy has undone me," she said mournfully, "and all is lost. Siena seed was my last hope. Without it, I don't know where to turn."

She refilled Xerxes' bowl with milk, and they left him gloom-ily lapping it up. Xerxes couldn't go back to Mrs. Pembroke with his nose the way it was. They trudged back to Nostradamus, whose fenders seemed to droop at their approach.

During the ride down Bald Mountain Road the atmosphere was as dismal inside the car as it was outside. Only once was the silence broken by any conversation.

"Are you going to try Dame Whirley again?" asked Fenton.

"Yes," said Mrs. Graymalkin, "though I fear it would be ex-pecting too much of her to . . . However, we shall see."

As they neared her friend's cottage Mrs. Graymalkin tooted Nostradamus's horn twice and did not jump the way the boys did when a horrendous hoot answered them.

"That would be Dame Whirley's pet owl, Athena. Athena is much better than any watchdog, if dear little Waldo will pardon my saying so. Keeps away all intruders."

"I can believe it," said Kerby.

Stopping the car, Mrs. Graymalkin teetered off toward the cottage and disappeared inside, and the earlier performance was repeated to the last detail. Chanting, caterwauling, screech-ing, huge smoke ring from the chimney, black cat around the house three times and in again —

"If that doesn't do the job I don't know what will," muttered Kerby.

The door opened and Mrs. Graymalkin teetered out. She

looked grim. As she opened the car door, she shook her head.

"Nothing."

This, then, was rock bottom. Never before had their friend visited Dame Whirley and come away completely empty-handed. For once, Mrs. Graymalkin seemed to have exhausted every hope.

The rest of the ride home was almost a blur. It was amazing, the speed an old car like Nostradamus seemed capable of making. They were back alongside the park in no time.

Mrs. Graymalkin turned to them with sad eyes and spoke the words they had dreaded.

"Well, Kerby and Fenton, and dear little Waldo, I am sorry that all the interesting experiences we have had together have to end this way . . ."

A great lump, so big it hurt like mad, formed like a fist in Kerby's throat.

"Won't we ever see you again?" he managed to ask.

"No, I very much fear that we . . . Well, I'll tell you what," she said, lifting her shoulders with a show of her old spirit, "I won't have to give up Nosy till Monday, because the contest won't be decided till then. So tomorrow night I shall try to drive over here for a few moments — though I fear I shall have no time for one last constitutional, much as I would love it — and we can say our good-byes then. That is, if you will be free to —"

"Easy!" cried Kerby, welcoming any respite from a final

farewell, even a mere twenty-four-hour postponement. "My folks are going out to dinner, and so are Fenton's, so he's coming over. We can be here — can't we, Fenton?"

"Sure!"

"Well, come if you can, and I shall do my very best not to disappoint you. Now, out you go, and let us hope for one last meeting tomorrow night at seven o'clock sharp!"

"We'll be here!"

They jumped out, said good night, and watched the old car whirl away around a corner.

Twenty-four hours, and then — good-bye forever!

It was almost more than they could stand.

7

WHEN KERBY SAID it would be easy for them to meet Mrs. Graymalkin Saturday night he thought he knew what he was talking about. But shortly before noon the roof fell in. Mrs. Maxwell came out on the back porch with one of those determined looks on her face mothers sometimes get. She smiled brightly.

"Boys, how would you like to make a lot of money?"

Kerby knew enough to be instantly wary.

"Huh?"

"How, Mrs. Maxwell?" asked Fenton in his usual polite way, but also on his guard.

"Well, Mrs. Gilbert phoned a minute ago, and she's in a terrible spot. She has to have a baby-sitter for Herbie tonight, but her regular sitter was busy, and now the one she got just phoned and said she was sick. So Mrs. Gilbert wondered if you boys could possibly fill in for her, and I said you could."

Everyone in their group howled but Waldo. Even Fenton, who would normally never have done such a thing.

"Baby-sit? We're not baby-sitters! We never have baby-sat and we don't want to start now!" cried Kerby.

Mrs. Maxwell folded her arms.

"Now, it won't hurt you boys a bit, you haven't a thing to do this evening, you were just going to stay home, and think of all the money you'll earn."

"But Fenton doesn't want to —"

"I've already called Fenton's mother and she agrees with me one hundred percent," said Mrs. Maxwell, cutting off that avenue of escape. "You know how many favors Mrs. Gilbert has done for all of us. It won't hurt either of you to do one little favor for her."

"One little favor!" groaned Kerby. If only his mother knew what she was asking! Yet he did not dare tell her. The last thing parents would ever understand was Mrs. Graymalkin — of that he and Fenton had long been certain. "Gee, Mom, Mrs. Gilbert is okay, but Herbie is a pain in the neck!"

"A monster!" agreed Fenton.

"Oh, for heaven's sake! If two great big boys can't handle one small child, then something's wrong. Now, I don't want to hear anything more about it. You're to eat your supper here and be over there by seven o'clock. She'll have Herbie ready for bed, and after you've read him one story you'll have the rest of the evening to do whatever you want. They have a lovely big color television set, and —"

There was no getting out of it. They were stuck with a baby-sitting job.

Moments later they were sitting in front of their clubhouse, trying to think.

"We can't be two places at once. We can't be over at Mrs. Gilbert's at seven sharp and meet Mrs. Graymalkin at seven sharp."

"Of course, *she* wasn't even sure she'd make it," Fenton pointed out. "She said she'd try not to disappoint us. But as long as there's even a chance of her coming, we've *got* to be there."

To miss that final meeting, to have Mrs. Graymalkin fade out of their lives while they baby-sat with Herbie Gilbert, was unthinkable. Of course, one of them could have gone and the other stayed with Herbie; but the idea of being the one who never saw her again was so unbearable that neither of them even mentioned such a possibility, though both thought of it.

As they talked, Kerby glanced in the direction of the street that ran in front of the vacant lot and saw a new source of annoyance approaching.

"Oh-oh, look who's coming down the street. Angie Morrissey. Get inside," he said, and slid into the clubhouse, closely followed by Fenton. "If she sees us she'll start it all over again, and I'm not in any mood to listen to *her* today."

"Or any other day," agreed Fenton.

Angie, who was a couple of years older than they, was their school's drama nut. She was already working on the school play for next year, to follow up the smash hit she had written last year. It was to be a comedy fantasy, with a large cast, and she wanted Fenton and Kerby to be in it. She wanted them to play two midgets!

"Midgets?" said Fenton when she first tried to talk them into it. "Are you crazy? For one thing, I'm too tall to be a midget."

"That's the joke!" said Angie. "Who ever heard of a tall midget? You'll get lots of laughs."

"I'll bet — all the wrong kind. Nothing doing!"

"You wait and see. You're going to be in my play, both of you."

"In a pig's eye!"

That was the way the discussion had gone, and Kerby wanted no more of it. Naturally, then, he was amazed when Fenton said, "Wait a minute. On second thought, I want to talk to Angie."

"What? Why?"

Fenton's eyes were narrowed in crafty calculation.

"She may be a pest, but she's also a baby-sitter," he said, and scrambled outside. "Hey, Angie!"

Kerby followed him as he loped across the lot to where Angie had stopped to look around at them.

"Hi, Fenton. Don't tell me, I can guess — you've changed your mind!"

"No, but — Listen, Angie, are you busy tonight?"

She gave him a teasing look.

"What are you trying to do, date me?"

"Aw, cut it out, Angie! I mean, are you baby-sitting?"

"No. In fact," she said angrily, "you're the guys who cut me out."

"Huh?"

"Aren't you sitting for Mrs. Gilbert tonight?"

"Yes — that is —"

"Well, she called me a few days ago and I told her I was already taken for tonight. Then this morning the one I was supposed to sit for had to cancel. So then I called Mrs. Gilbert in case she still needed me, but she said she was trying you because you would be able to sit for her regularly. I think she was sore because I took another job first without finding out if she wanted me."

"What? You mean, *you're* her regular sitter?"

"I *was*. But now, the heck with her! She's all yours. I wouldn't sit for her now if she *begged* me. Well, maybe if she begged me, but only then."

"Then we'll get her to beg you!" cried Fenton desperately, and then, too late, caught himself. "What I mean is, we've got something else we'd just as leave do, so —"

Angie eyed him shrewdly.

"Oh? Okay. I'll tell you what. If you can get her to call me up and beg me to take your place, then I'll come."

"Great!"

"*But* — only if you both promise to be in my play."

"Hey, now! That's no fair!"

"Okay, then, forget it."

"Wait! We didn't say no —"

"Then say yes."

Looking at each other did not help Kerby and Fenton. They knew they were hooked.

"Well . . . okay."

Angie grinned broadly.

"It's a deal. But remember, she's got to call me herself and beg a little."

"Okay," said Fenton. "We'll work it somehow."

8

KERBY WAITED till Angie had strutted away. Then he asked the burning question.

"How?"

"How what?"

"You said we'll work it somehow. How?"

"Give me time! There's got to be a way."

How to force a grown woman to beg a teenage girl to change her mind. It was a large order. They thought long and hard, but got nowhere. After a while they drifted back to Kerby's house. His mother was in the kitchen, putting onions through a grinder for something she was getting ready for Sunday. When they came in her eyes were watering, and in a couple of seconds so were theirs.

"Whew! Let's get out of here!" said Kerby. "I don't see how you stand it, Mom!"

"I don't either," said Mrs. Maxwell. "These onions are really fierce."

The boys rushed outside again. They were hardly in the

backyard, however, before Fenton snapped his fingers and began smiling through his tears.

"I've got it!"

A quarter to seven found the boys hurrying toward the Gilbert house with Waldo at their heels. Just before they got there they slipped behind a hedge and Fenton took a round object out of his pocket. It was an onion that had been cut in half. He handed half to Kerby.

In a moment their eyes were streaming.

"Wow! That stings!"

They tossed the onion behind a bush. Fenton took out a pepper shaker and flipped pepper into the air.

"Take a deep breath. Okay, let's go! Waldo, you stay out here and wait!"

Mrs. Gilbert opened her door to find two watery-eyed boys waiting outside, both of whom sneezed soon after entering the house.

"Good heavens! Don't tell me that —"

Fenton coughed dismally.

"I guess we've caught something, Mrs. Gilbert," he said in a most apologetic tone of voice. "We don't know whether it's a cold or some new kind of flu, but —"

"Good grief! I can't let you boys get near *Herbie!*" wailed Mrs. Gilbert. Of all the neighborhood mothers she was well known as the champion worrier. Herbie was a fat little brat

56

with an iron constitution, but she was convinced he was very delicate. She collapsed into a chair. "Oh, what am I going to do *now?"*

"Well, we knew we couldn't sit for you, so we scouted around and found out that Angie Morrissey is free tonight —"

"Angie?" Mrs. Gilbert looked ready to weep. "That would be my luck! I'm sure she wouldn't come now, just to spite me!"

"What?" said Fenton innocently. "But why would she —"

Mrs. Gilbert's eyes shifted around in a guilty way.

"Well, I'm afraid I was rather short with Angie on the phone earlier today when I thought — er — that is —"

"Oh, gosh, Mrs. Gilbert, Angie isn't somebody to hold a grudge. I'll bet if you called her up and told her what a spot you're in —"

"I'd get down on my knees if she'd come!"

"That ought to do it!" cried Kerby, and then added hastily, "What I mean is, if you call her up I'm sure she'll come."

Mrs. Gilbert decided to try. She dialed Angie's number, waited, and frowned.

"It's busy."

Kerby and Fenton shot a burning glance at each other, full of anger and despair. Angie was supposed to be expecting the call! But maybe she'd got tired of waiting. Maybe she'd given up and phoned a girl friend. Maybe someone else in the large Morrissey family had settled down for a nice long gossip.

Mrs. Gilbert tried again.

Waited.

Spoke.

"Hello! May I speak to Angie, please?"

Across the room a grandfather's clock cleared its throat and struck seven. Was Mrs. Graymalkin sitting in Nostradamus alongside the park, waiting? Had she come at all?

Mrs. Gilbert all but knelt in front of the phone. Angie graciously consented to come over and save the day. But all of that took more time. But finally, after being thanked profusely, the boys were able to escape. They left Mrs. Gilbert spraying germ-killer all over the living room.

They were fifteen minutes late getting to the park, and when they arrived no ancient sedan was waiting at the curb. They stood on the corner across from the park, staring at emptiness, and for a moment neither of them spoke. Waldo looked up at them and whimpered.

"She couldn't wait," said Fenton finally.

"Maybe she never came."

They hung around for a few minutes, but without any real hope.

"*She* wouldn't be late. When has she ever been late, Kerby?"

"I know. But I sure wish . . . Well, come on, we might as well go home. Darn that onion juice, it still hurts!"

"We used too much of it," agreed Fenton, rubbing at the corners of his eyes.

58

9

THERE IS NOTHING worse than being burdened with a great sorrow and having nothing to do but think about it. That was the spot Kerby and Fenton were in now. The events of the evening had left them completely at loose ends, with nowhere to go and nothing to do. Trudging home by way of the vacant lot, they sat down listlessly in front of their clubhouse. The melancholy haze of the twilight hour matched their mood exactly.

For want of something better, Kerby dug up an old bone of contention.

"Well, now that it's all over, you've got to admit one thing," he said. "You've got to admit Mrs. Graymalkin *is* a witch."

"I'll admit nothing of the sort," snapped Fenton. "Why do you say that, anyway? If there *were* such things — which there aren't — and she *were* one — which she isn't — then why would she have to put up with all this trouble? She'd just wave a wand, and —"

"You're forgetting she's got another witch working against

her, a mean witch, that old Dame Whoever-she-is, and it looks like she's been too much for her."

Fenton squirmed around irritably, and glared at Kerby, but for once he had no comeback. He wanted to think of an answer to that one, but was too depressed to try. He got to his feet.

"Let's go!"

"Where?"

"Oh, anywhere, I don't care."

"What'll we do?"

"I don't know!"

They had turned away from the clubhouse to go somewhere to do something, they didn't know where or what, when a sound made them whirl around.

A horn was tooting, a familiar horn. Across the vacant lot at the curb stood a tall, gaunt old sedan they had never expected to see again.

"Mrs. Graymalkin! My gosh, we thought you —"

"We were late getting to the park, and —"

"Roo-o-o-o-o!"

"Yes, yes, yes, I can well understand, because I was late, *dreadfully* late myself, and for the most extraordinary reason. Oh, how fortunate it is that I happened to look for you in the right place!"

As she beamed down at them from the car they could see,

below the broad brim of her floppy black hat, a crisscross of adhesive tape holding a bandage on her forehead.

"What happened to you?" cried Kerby. "What's the matter with your head?"

"That's part of my story. Jump in, jump in, and I'll tell you all!"

They jumped in and were scarcely settled on the back seat before Nostradamus was flapping away down the street.

"Did you find out anything from your books, Mrs. Graymalkin?" Fenton asked hopefully.

"No. Since last night I have spent every moment in my library — all in vain. At last it was time to come to the park to say good-bye to you. I creaked out of my chair, weary and sore of limb. And at that moment, Nemo acted."

"Nemo?"

"My pet raven. Nemo, as usual, was perched on the very top of my bookshelves — which are quite high, quite high. As I rose he kicked a large bundle of parchment scrolls over the edge of the shelf, a bundle I had quite forgotten was there."

"And it hit you on the head?"

"Precisely. And with no gentle impact. I was stunned. It took me a moment to collect myself, after which I was forced to waste precious minutes bandaging my head. I returned to the library prepared to give Nemo a good scolding — but then I had second thoughts on the matter. Instead of scolding Nemo

I gathered up the scrolls and went through them one by one . . ."

"And did you find something?"

"Yes! From one of those ancient scrolls that have lain undisturbed for — well, for many a long year — I learned secrets that could give us another chance, if only they prove to be true!"

The boys cheered and Waldo rooooed. *Any* chance was better than none!

Then it occurred to them what "another chance" probably involved.

Saturday night on Bald Mountain!

It was a shivery thought, but after all they had been through, they felt ready for anything, even that.

Which was just as well.

"One vitally important thing I learned," said Mrs. Graymalkin as they spun around Carlsen Circle, "is that more than one variety of frightweed may grow on Bald Mountain. There is a somewhat different variety for which conditions are favorable there, and it is one which would explain Xerxes' nasal affliction. Fortunately, it also produces a quite acceptable type of siena seed.

"So it may be that what Xerxes found and ate was not the shy denizen of small caves, *Pimpinella troglodytes,* but the other variety, and that Xerxes was merely hiding in the cave owing to self-consciousness about his appearance. And here we are!"

Once again they swerved into Bald Mountain Road and were jouncing up, up the narrow lane. Once again, darkness seemed to rush down to meet them. Dame Whirley's cottage went by, and then the cemetery.

"Not much farther now," said Mrs. Graymalkin as the great writhing trees closed in around them on each side of the winding road. " 'Skulls of scapegoats, one on three —' Yes, yes, there they are, and now of course we are not frightened enough this time for 'Double beat of pounding heart,' but then we no longer need to time ourselves anyway because now we *know* where to stop!"

Nostradamus jolted to a halt. Mrs. Graymalkin switched off the headlights. They sat in a fuzzy gray-black gloom.

"The moon is much brighter tonight. No need to waste electricity. Now, who wants to run down the path and fetch poor Xerxes? His presence is essential."

There was a noticeable lack of volunteers.

"I don't think Xerxes would listen to me —"

"Me, either!"

Mrs. Graymalkin cackled mischievously.

"I was only teasing. I doubt it will be necessary."

"M-r-r-r-ow?"

"There — you see? Thanks to his keen ears he heard us coming. And no doubt he is famished again."

Sure enough, Xerxes was outside, nose aglow, tail in the air, mewing and purring. Mrs. Graymalkin once again produced supplies from beneath her cape, and Xerxes was soon lapping away with great gusto.

"And a spoonful of cod-liver oil will not go amiss, I'll warrant. Good for the fur," she said, bringing forth a bottle and spoon. Kerby made a face.

"Yuk! Cats will eat anything!"

"A spoonful wouldn't hurt either of *you,* for that matter," she countered tartly. "However, I won't insist. Everybody out, now! The instant Xerxes has finished his milk we shall begin our ascent of Hangman's Knob."

10

HER WORDS FELL like a thunderbolt on the boys.

"Where? Do what?"

She gave them an imperious glance.

"Our quest beckons us to higher ground. The rare species of frightweed we seek can only be found where — Well, never mind, our course is unmistakable. Our path is clear."

Staring fearfully up the grim slope that faced them, Kerby and Fenton felt their path was anything but clear. All they could see was a scratch through the brambles. And at the top, somewhere at the top of that narrow path . . . Hangman's Knob?

"No g-g-groups this time?" asked Kerby in a reedy voice. If it was going to be group activities again, count him out!

"No, no, no, we shall all start up together. Are you finished, Xerxes? Very well — lead the way!" said Mrs. Graymalkin, and Xerxes sprang away up the difficult path. He moved with an obedient alacrity that made Kerby and Fenton wonder what else might have been in that cod-liver oil. After a single surprised stare Waldo trotted after the cat.

The boys followed, glancing back frequently to make sure Mrs. Graymalkin was coming. Then all at once they came out into the open, and there above them was a great, bald, wind-swept knob of rock. A few weedy patches of black earth here and there dotted the boulders and ledges.

At the very crest of the knob, silhouetted against a full moon, stood a tall square timber topped by a horizontal bar.

"What's that?"

"Why, that's the gibbet, Kerby, dear," said Mrs. Graymalkin. "That is what criminals were hanged from in olden times — criminals, and quite a number of poor innocent wretches, according to the legend."

"What legend?" asked Fenton in hushed tones.

"Well, it seems that a number of the persons who were hanged here were later found to have been innocent. This preyed on the hangman's mind. As a result, the last person he hanged on that gibbet was — himself."

While this was sinking in, Mrs. Graymalkin whisked from under her black cape a seemingly ancient scroll of parchment and unrolled it.

"Mind you, we are not here simply to learn fascinating side-lights of our country's early history. All this has a direct bearing on our search for *Pimpinella suicidus.*"

"*Suicidus?*"

"Yes. A Latin term. Listen to what this age-old document tells us in reference to the growing habits of this species of frightweed."

In a croaking chant she read from the scroll:

Pimpinella Suicidus

Where hangman sways
Who tried his ways
On bones
He owns,
Enough for a feast
May be found by a beast
With a nose
That glows
Like a spark
In the dark.

She gave them a glittering glance.

"So you see, we have come to the right place. So now you must run, run, run to the top and observe carefully the search being made by —"

"What? Why do we have to go any farther? Can't Xerxes do his searching without *us?*"

"Yes — but you must be ready to snatch away the prize, when found."

Kerby's teeth might well have begun chattering had it not been that — well, with Mrs. Graymalkin there to give them courage . . .

"Well, okay, Mrs. Graymalkin, let's go."

"*You* go," she replied. "I shall remain here to cover our retreat — if needs be."

A large jagged icicle replaced Kerby's spine, and his teeth made up for lost time. Go up there *alone?* With their strange friend staying behind "to cover their retreat — if needs be," whatever that might mean? Why should they need to have their retreat covered? What would they be retreating from? "Where hangman sways . . ." Did that mean . . . ?

"Xerxes, Waldo! Kerby! Fenton! Away, away, before it's too late!" ordered Mrs. Graymalkin in a stern tone that brooked no delay. Almost before they knew what they were doing they were scrambling up the bald knob, dodging around the rough boulders, with their hearts in their throats.

The animals outpaced them. When the boys reached the top, Xerxes and Waldo were nowhere to be seen. Kerby wanted to call out but was too frightened to make a sound. Fenton was in the same condition. Ahead of them, rearing up larger and larger, blacker and blacker against the moon, towered the sinister gibbet with its dreadful crossbar.

Always a game one, Fenton found the courage to whisper a few words.

"Look around. If we see any funny-looking kind of weed we'll pick some."

Glad to look anywhere but at the gibbet, Kerby tore his eyes away from it and fixed them on the ground. He and Fenton were both searching hard when gradually they became aware that the moonlight had dimmed slightly, as though a film of cloud were passing over it. They glanced up.

At the end of a dark line that dropped from the crossbar of the gibbet a shadowy form swayed gently to and fro, a form with arms and dangling legs . . .

They screamed and ran, tearing down the gravelly surface with a speed that made small rocks fly together and strike sparks.

"Mrs. Graymalkin! Help!"

"Boys!" Suddenly she was in front of them, stern and forbidding. "Why did you leave the field?"

They skidded to a stop and blurted words breathlessly.

"We — we saw —"

"Look!"

She was pointing behind them. They turned to look.

Xerxes was springing down the rocky knob, but he was bringing nothing with him. No weeds protruded from his mouth below his glowing nose. A horrible feeling of guilt overwhelmed Kerby. Had they left Xerxes at just the wrong moment? Had he found the precious frightweed and gobbled it all *again*? Was their last, slim hope gone?

"Look!"

Once again Mrs. Graymalkin was pointing a fateful finger. Once again they looked.

Bounding down the slope came Waldo. In his mouth he was carrying a straggly bunch of weeds. They looked as if they were on fire, but they were not. The red glow came from Waldo's nose.

11

"BRAVO, WALDO! I can always count on you!" cried Mrs. Graymalkin. She seized the clump of weed Waldo held up to her and raised it high.

"Our only hope, siena seed, in Nostradamus's hour of need!" she crooned, then lowered it to eye level and took a good practical look at it. "Yes, yes, yes, enough siena seed here for a nice batch of cookies."

From beneath the black cape she brought out a small transparent bag, packed the weeds carefully inside it, and stowed the bag away again. None of the others were paying any attention, however. They all had concerns of their own.

Kerby and Fenton were staring dumbfounded at Waldo's nose.

Waldo was squinting at it cross-eyed. He had supposed the red glow to come from the weeds. But now that he had yielded them to Mrs. Graymalkin the glow was still with him. Very much with him. His eyes, still crossed, widened with horror.

Xerxes was also staring at Waldo's nose. And suddenly Xerxes collapsed in a merry heap, beating the ground with his paws and making sounds as though he were being tickled to death.

Waldo bared his fangs and barked angrily, but Mrs. Graymalkin said, "Now, now, tit for tat is only fair. You had a good laugh at Xerxes' expense, now it's his turn."

Waldo stared up at her with a how-could-you expression. If his faith in her could be shaken, it was shaken now.

"My gosh, this is worse instead of better!" cried Kerby, accurately echoing Waldo's own thoughts. "How come *Waldo* ends up with a red nose, too? Xerxes was supposed to find the frightweed!"

"Or at least, so you thought," murmured Mrs. Graymalkin.

"But *he* was the one who already had a nose that glows like a spark in the dark!"

"Well, I fear the ancient verses are a bit ambiguous, Kerby, dear. Fenton will tell us what 'ambiguous' means."

Fenton pulled himself together enough to answer.

"I think it means something that can be taken two ways."

"Correct as usual, Fenton, dear. The point is, what the verses actually mean is that a beast — an animal — has a nose that glows like a spark in the dark *after* it has found the frightweed and consumed a portion of it."

"What? You mean Waldo ate — But why would he?"

"He probably did not intend to, but in the excitement of the

75

discovery he no doubt inadvertently swallowed a few morsels of siena seed. At any rate, everything worked out beautifully, just as I had hoped."

What? Had they heard aright?

"You mean you deliberately let Waldo get a red nose?" cried Fenton, shocked to the core.

She looked down at them quizzically.

"You mean, how could I do such a thing to dear little Waldo, my best four-footed friend in all the world?"

She flung up a bony finger.

"All part of my master plan!"

"Your what?"

"My master plan. It was the only way to save poor Xerxes."

They had been dumbfounded. Now they were dumberfounded. Especially Waldo. He sank to the ground with his head between his paws and whimpered. If there was one thing he had never expected to be, it was the savior of Xerxes — especially at the price of a red glowing nose.

Kerby put Waldo's question into words for him.

"But how is his red nose going to help Xerxes?"

"Ah-ha! Let us learn how that can be! Let us listen to ancient words once more!" Again she whipped out the parchment scroll. "Listen to this!" she ordered, and read:

Thrice around the hangman's house
Dog by cat must ridden be,
Thrice around the hangman's house
Cat on dog must ride with glee;
Eye for eye,
Tooth for tooth —
Nose for nose
Is also truth!

While Kerby's spine experienced the Return of the Icicle and his teeth did a castanet encore, Mrs. Graymalkin rolled up the scroll and restored it to its place under her black cape.

"We must give it a try," she said, "we must give it a try."

The boys' eyes were rolling in all directions.

"The h-hangman's house? Where's that?"

"Just a few paces down the slope on the other side of the gibbet. You can't miss it."

"What do you mean, *we* can't miss it?" shrilled Kerby.

"Well, I really wouldn't care to pass by the gibbet. I hate the nasty thing!"

"I'm not crazy about it myself!" cried Kerby. "You mean to say we've got to go up there *again* —"

"Past that gibbet to a h-h —"

Fenton stopped just in time — or almost. In his nervous state he had nearly said something unscientific. He stopped, but even then Mrs. Graymalkin picked him up on it.

"Were you going to say a 'haunted house,' Fenton, dear?" she asked in an innocent voice but with a wicked twinkle in her eye. "A mere slip of the tongue, I am sure — we know very well that you don't believe in such nonsense as ghosts, don't we, Fenton?"

Kerby cried, "But we saw something — something — something black, but see-through black, hanging on the gibbet!"

"A mere trick of the light," said Mrs. Graymalkin in her airiest manner. "You expected to see some such thing, so naturally you saw it. This time, as you pass by, don't give it so much as a single glance. Be firm!"

"We'll be firmer if you come along!"

"No, really, there are historical associations involved that would make it most intolerable for me to — Now, now, we mustn't delay any longer — away you go! The sooner ancient wise words are heeded the sooner we may all be on the road to recovery. And when you reach the hangman's house, do not let incidental noises bother you — old cottages creak so in the wind! Once the deed is done, carry Xerxes and Waldo back here and we will soon be on our way home!"

"*Carry* them back?"

"Never fear, all will come clear! Now go!"

In the meantime her words had been sinking in elsewhere.

> *Thrice around the hangman's house*
> *Dog by cat must ridden be,*
> *Thrice around the hangman's house*
> *Cat on dog must ride with glee!* . . .

Waldo and Xerxes stared at each other. Then Waldo put his head back and howled, while Xerxes, purring, walked over to a tree and began sharpening his claws.

12

WHEN MRS. GRAYMALKIN gave orders in a certain tone of voice there was no getting out of it. The boys knew it, Waldo knew it, and Xerxes was catching on fast. They moved out, the boys first, then Xerxes, and finally, grudging every step he took, Waldo.

Once more they walked up the stony slope toward the ghastly gibbet, silhouetted now against the lower half of the moon.

"Remember," muttered Fenton, "don't look at that thing when we're going by."

Suddenly a cold wind howled across the dreary summit, turning their nervous perspiration to ice crystals. Stumbling on as fast as they could go, both boys did their utmost to keep their eyes straight ahead.

Now they were near, very near. Something dimmed the moon-light . . .

"Don't look, Kerby!"

"I won't!"

Shielding his eyes with both hands Kerby raced along beside

80

Fenton across the crest of Hangman's Knob and down the far slope.

Fenton slid to a stop on the pebbly ground and pointed ahead. "Look!"

Just a few paces below, as Mrs. Graymalkin had said, stood a dark cottage with broken windows and a door hanging at an odd angle from its hinges.

Kerby gulped, then turned to Waldo and Xerxes.

"Hurry up, you two! You know what to do — get going! I'm not going to hang around — er — *stay* around here any longer than I have to!"

Waldo made a noise that sounded like a bad word in dog language. How true the ancient saying that pride goeth before the fall! Only last night he had watched with superior canine scorn while a black cat had made three undignified circuits of a house, yowling all the way.

His glowing red nose twitching in anticipation, Xerxes strolled to the cottage and stood waiting. Letting out a big sigh, the condemned dog followed.

Before Waldo knew it Xerxes had leaped onto his back. After a single yelp of horrified surprise Waldo remembered what had to be done and took off around the corner of the house.

Waldo's howling and Xerxes' yowling were bad enough, but then something was added to the uproar that curdled the boys' blood. From inside the house came wails and moans and shrieks.

"Old cottages c-creak in the w-w-wind," Fenton reminded Kerby, but Kerby wasn't having any of that.

"I know creaking when I hear it, and that's not creaking!"

Round the far corner of the house came the howling, yowling pair, and only the sight of them kept Kerby from bolting. Round they came again, and then —

"Thrice," said Fenton. "Here they come for the third time . . ."

With Xerxes still claw-fastened to his back Waldo shot into sight and headed for the finish line.

ZAP!

A bolt of static electricity crackled from nose to nose. Xerxes

flew off Waldo's back into the air and landed in a bush. Waldo tumbled forward and sprawled in the dust, a lifeless form.

Kerby rushed to his side.

"Waldo! . . . He's not dead! He's still breathing!"

Fenton plunged into the bushes. He returned carrying a limp Xerxes.

"He's still breathing, too," reported Fenton.

"Mrs. Graymalkin said to carry them back. She *knew* this would happen!"

"And their noses are okay now. When they blacked out, so did their noses. Bring Waldo and let's get out of here!"

The hangman's house was as silent now as though never a sound had made the night hideous. Hurrying back with Waldo and Xerxes the boys were so preoccupied that they even forgot to be frightened of the gibbet. When they happened to glance that way they saw only the wooden frame standing stark on the summit.

Mrs. Graymalkin quickly relieved their concern for Waldo and Xerxes.

"Fear not, the poor dears have merely suffered a slight, quite harmless concussion. By the time I let you out beside your beloved vacant lot they will be as good as new. Now, if only my siena seed cookies turn out well — I *do* hope I won't burn them — there may be cause for hope. I have learned my lesson about one thing, however," she added grimly.

"What's that?"

"I must not let my rival have the slightest suspicion I may have found an alternative to my dinglenut puffs. I dare not suggest a private preview of our entries amongst our own circle now — there is no telling what new mischief she might then be capable of. No, I must enter them straightaway in the newspaper's contest. I don't like it, but there is no way out of it now. Very well, then — it shall be done!"

By the time Nostradamus stopped beside the vacant lot both Waldo and Xerxes were sitting up and yawning. And when they realized they no longer had those stoplight snoots they were a happy pair.

In the meantime, however, a worrisome thought had occurred to Fenton.

"I don't see how you can expect to win first prize if the judges who try your cookies end up with red noses!"

Mrs. Graymalkin whooped merrily.

"What a picture! And a tempting one, I must admit. However, have no fear. Fortunately siena seed no longer has that effect once it has been baked. Now, here we are, and away you go!"

"Okay. Good night, Mrs. Graymalkin — and good luck with your cookies!" said Fenton.

"We'll be rooting for you!" said Kerby.

"Thank you, boys, thank you! Remember, Monday evening's newspaper will give the results of the contest. I shall save Nosy if I possibly can!"

With a wave from Mrs. Graymalkin and a fender-flap from Nostradamus they were gone, leaving the boys to wonder if they would ever see either of them again.

There was no time to stand around sighing, however. It was important to get home as fast as they could, before any of them were seen, especially Xerxes. Together the four of them ran across the vacant lot and slipped through the fence into Kerby's backyard.

Once there Xerxes stopped and turned. He and Waldo eyed each other. Then, all of a sudden, Xerxes reared up on his hind legs. He put his paws to his ears, waggled his claws at Waldo, stuck out his tongue, and yowled joyously.

"M-R-R-R-O-W-W!"

"R-R-R-R-O-O-O-F!"

They were off. Xerxes yowling, Waldo barking, through the hedge they went, and up the tree went Xerxes. In mere seconds the back door of Mrs. Pembroke's house was thrown open. Waldo tiptoed home.

"Xerxes! Xerxes, is that you?" said Mrs. Pembroke in a quivering voice, as though hardly daring to hope.

"Meow?" replied Xerxes in his tenderest tones.

The rest of the reunion was so sickening and baby-talkish that Kerby had to put his hands over his ears and rush inside the house.

13

IT TOOK THEM half of Sunday to convince their mothers that their "colds" were not bad enough to keep them in bed. Kerby could hear Mrs. Pembroke singing in her backyard as she gardened. She was so happy she even baked some brownies and brought them over for Kerby and Fenton when she heard they were sick.

"And she didn't even put poison in them," as Kerby remarked later to Fenton.

Monday afternoon they went over to the corner drugstore hoping to get an early edition of the paper, but it was late coming. They hung around the store while the day waned and afternoon shadows lengthened. Finally the stack of papers appeared. They bought a copy and pawed it open, looking for the food page.

"Here it is!" cried Fenton. "The winner — Oh, nuts!"

DAME KITTY HARLING'S
MYSTERY ANISE SEED COOKIES

"Dame Kitty Harling! That must be her worst enemy!"

"Of course it is!" Fenton was crushed. "I can't believe it!"

The recipe was given. It included something called "mystery anise seed." The story quoted one of the judges as saying, "We don't know where Dame Kitty gets her mystery anise seed but we'd give a lot to know. It's marvelous!"

Overwhelmed, stricken, they trudged away toward home.

"I'll bet she burned her cookies," groaned Kerby. "She was worried about that."

Even Waldo caught something of the prevailing misery. It was without his usual light step that he plodded on ahead to make an automatic inspection of the clubhouse.

Then Fenton stopped in his tracks, looking thoughtful.

"What's the matter, Fenton?"

"Well . . . maybe it doesn't mean anything, but I just thought of something that's kind of odd."

"What?"

"Anise. Change the letters around and it spells 'siena.'"

Up ahead of them Waldo stuck his head out of the clubhouse and barked urgently. Something was up. The boys broke into a run.

Inside the clubhouse Waldo was nosing a box. It was a brand new box labeled ANAGRAMS.

Fenton smote his forehead.

"I've got it!"

He yanked the lid off the box, set it on the ground, and with trembling fingers began picking out letters and lining them up on the box top.

"*She* put this here for us! Look at this!"

He arranged letters so that they spelled:

DAME   KITTY   HARLING

"Now! We take the E and D from D A M E, the I and T from K I T T Y, the H from H A R L I N G—"

"E-D-I-T-H T.— GRAYMALKIN!" shouted Kerby.

Fenton sat back on his haunches, overcome by admiration.

"That is the greatest anagram I ever saw!" he said reverently. "She used Dame Kitty Harling as an alias because she didn't want to use her real name! Come on!"

They reached the park just in time. Nostradamus was pulling away from the curb. But as the old car disappeared down the street its left rear fender definitely tossed off an extra flap, while a bony hand was thrust out the window in a triumphant wave. The boys waved wildly, and grinned at each other, while Waldo threw his head back in a victory howl.

"We're back in business," said Kerby.

It was a grand feeling.